my princesses
learn to share

written by **Amie Carlson**　　illustrated by **Heather Heyworth**

TYNDALE KIDS

Tyndale House Publishers, Inc. | Carol Stream, IL

Visit Tyndale's website for kids at www.tyndale.com/kids.

TYNDALE is a registered trademark of Tyndale House Publishers, Inc.

The Tyndale Kids logo is a trademark of Tyndale House Publishers, Inc.

My Princesses Learn to Share

Copyright © 2014 Tyndale House Publishers, Inc.

Illustrations by Heather Heyworth. Copyright © by Tyndale House Publishers, Inc. All rights reserved.

Designed by Jacqueline L. Nuñez

Edited by Stephanie Rische

Scripture quotations are taken from the *Holy Bible*, New Living Translation, copyright © 1996, 2004, 2007, 2013 by Tyndale House Foundation. Used by permission of Tyndale House Publishers, Inc., Carol Stream, Illinois 60188. All rights reserved.

For manufacturing information regarding this product, please call 1-800-323-9400.

ISBN 978-1-4143-9662-0

Printed in China

20   19   18   17   16   15   14

7   6   5   4   3   2   1

What makes a princess?
I'd sure like to know.
Could I be a princess?
I wish it were so!

It's there in the Bible,
So I know that it's true.
We are God's children—
You and me, too!

Since God is our Father,
The King up above,
We are all princesses,
The ones that he loves!

See how
very much
our Father loves us,
for he calls us
his children,
and that is
what we are!

1 John 3:1

Princess Hope was in her bedroom in the tall tower of her castle. She had a big day ahead of her—first a feast in the dining hall and then a dance with the prince! It was time to pick out something to wear for the ball. . . .

"I love playing princesses," Hope said as she sorted through the giant box of dress-up clothes.

3   "Me, too," Grace said. "And our moms said we get to play all afternoon!"

Hope held up her favorite dress and tried to pull it out of the box. She gave it a tug and then realized that Grace was holding on to the other side.

4

"That's my dress," Hope said. "You can wear the blue one."

"I don't want to wear the blue one. I want the pink sparkly one!" Grace said. "You get to wear the pink one every day."

5

Hope tugged the dress again. "Let go—it's mine!"

"But I want it. YOU let go."

"Give it to me, or I won't play with you anymore!" Hope stuck out her bottom lip.

RRRRRRIIIIIPP!

"Oh, no!" the girls shouted.

7

Hope's mom stuck her head through the door. "What's going on in here?"

"Grace ripped my dress!"

"I did not! You wouldn't let me wear it."

Hope's mom reached out to the girls and gave each of them a hug. "Girls, have you heard the story in the Bible about the little boy who shared his lunch with Jesus?"

"One day Jesus was talking to thousands of people about God's love and how they could learn to follow him," she said. "It was a long, hot day, and at lunchtime, Jesus' disciples came to him. 'We don't know how we're going to feed everyone,' they said. All they had was the lunch a little boy had brought with him."

"It would have been perfectly fine for the boy to keep his lunch for himself," Hope's mom went on. "But he wanted to give his lunch to Jesus to share with everyone. He only had five loaves of bread and two fish, but Jesus did a miracle! Somehow there was enough food for everyone to eat and feel full."

"Now girls, what do you think would have happened if the boy hadn't shared his food?"

"The crowd wouldn't have gotten lunch?" Hope said.

13

"Well, Jesus would have been able to find another way to feed everyone. He is God, and he can do anything. But if he hadn't shared, the little boy wouldn't have had a chance to be a part of the miracle!"

"Hope, I'm very sorry your favorite dress got ripped," Mom said. "But I think a true princess would have shared her dress with her guest. Don't you?"

Hope frowned. "But I wanted the prettiest one."

"I know you wanted to be the prettiest princess," Hope's mom said. "But being beautiful isn't about what you wear on the outside. What really matters is being beautiful on the inside. God's princesses share with their friends, and that's what makes them beautiful."

16

Hope and Grace went to the kitchen, where Hope's mom had a snack for them. While they ate, Hope's mom sewed a pretty pink patch onto the sparkly pink dress. She handed the dress to Hope.

Right away, Hope handed the dress to Grace. "You can be the pink princess today. I want to share with you."

19

"Will you join me for tea, Princess Grace?"

"Of course, your highness," Grace said. And the girls played happily ever after until it was time to go to the ball.

Don't forget to do good and to share.

—Hebrews 13:16

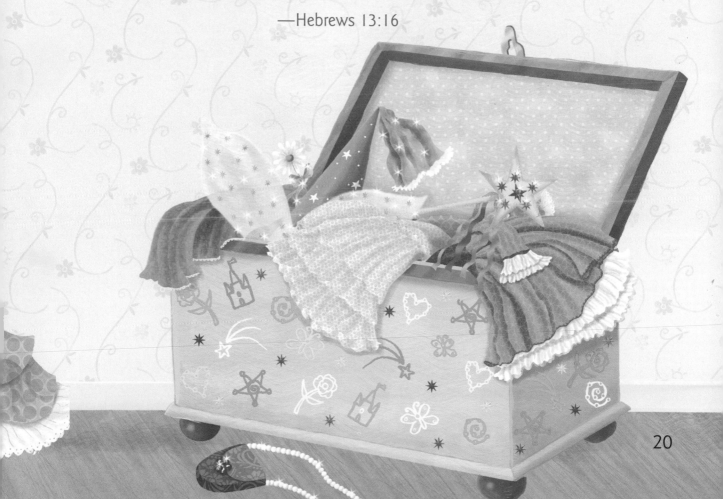

Amie Carlson is a freelance writer who has contributed to *365 Pocket Prayers for Mothers* and *Relevant* magazine and written for Willow Creek Community Church and the Willow Creek Association. She is the mother of two grown children who loved to play dress-up when they were little. She came up with the idea for this story in a brainstorming session with her daughter, Molly, while sitting outside Panera on a sunny, summer afternoon, remembering hours of giggling fun and little-girl drama from playdates filled with piles of well-loved dress-up clothes.

Heather Heyworth lives and works in a sleepy Suffolk town in the United Kingdom. After graduating from Goldsmiths, University of London, with a diploma in art and design, she became creative manager at a design studio and then art editor at a greeting card publisher.

Her introduction to the world of children's books came when she illustrated, designed, and copublished her own licensed-character activity books. Since then, she has illustrated many titles, including picture books, board books, and educational books. She loves creating new characters, especially "butterfly princesses" who flutter around her imagination, scattering magical fairy dust as they go.